CW00498086

Short Stories

Tne Main Words

Ekaterina Yakovina

The main words

The book lay on the table. The big empty house had only one table and the book lay on it. The windows were opened. A fresh wind blew from the windows to the open door. Silence. I listened. Only the music of leaves from the open windows. I went to the table with interest.

I thought, "This house reminds me of a space of memories. We want to catch our memories. They play with us like the fresh wind which is amusing itself with my interest in the book."

The book had the title "For You." I opened it. Nothing… I could not understand what was the meaning of the book.

"If it is for me then I should receive some information by reading this book," I thought. "An empty house and an empty book… Perhaps I should write something in the book? I think it should be the most important thing in my life. Maybe I should write the serious thoughts which often come to me."

I did not know. I went to the open window. A big green field laid before my eyes. Small yellow flowers looked up at me. Who could give me the answer about the strange book? I was alone. The house was empty. The book had not anything that could help me. I returned to the table. I decided to write all I would like to write in that strange book.

"I have complete freedom," I thought. "Full freedom is a rarity. I should make good use of it."

"I love you," I wrote.

Those words were my first words. I thought that I would begin a long story about my love which was very important in my life. But no. I did not have the words to describe my feeling.

"What is it? Where is the flight of my words which always help me to talk with people?"

I love you …

The words were flying above the big green field. A ray of the warm sun took the words and the house was empty again. "I love you" were the only words which were written on the first page of the book. Suddenly I felt that I was tired of the empty house and the white empty pages of the book and my wish to write something. I lost the desire to add something to these words. It was all that I could write in the book. It was full both of joy and sadness at the same time. I closed the book and went to the door. The fresh air was glad to take my body in its embrace. I received another freedom by the space of the field and high sky.

"This is really the freedom for me," I thought.

"I do not need to write about my feelings and thoughts in the book. I will save my spiritual world only for me."

I was full of true emotions at that moment. I was full of own sky and memories. I closed the door of the empty house and continued on the way of my life.

It was not the end of this strange adventure with me. Much later I returned to the house. Many years of my life had passed. I was not young. The door of the strange house was opened as it had been many years ago. The field was green and beautiful. I noticed that the house had grown much older. The book still laid on the table of the empty old house.

"For you," I read again. I opened the book.

The phrase "I love you" was written by many different people. I found no other words upon the pages. The book was not empty. People who had visited the house had written the words which were the most important for them. No one had been able to find any words which could be added to the clarity of these tender words.

The book was written. The house was full of beauty and a hope. I closed the book. I closed the door of the house. I understood that the most important of our feelings lived in the space of fresh wind and the warm smile of the sun. They cannot be spoken in the usual language of people.

I love you.

The yellow bird

Daniel opened his eyes.

There were colored walls and a high black ceiling in a strange room where he found himself. He opened a blue window. A soundless white space was flying outside the window. It was a space of emptiness. Daniel closed the window quickly because that white emptiness gave him a feeling of horror.

"I will stay inside this colored room until somebody explains for me the situation," he decided.

He waited several minutes but nobody came into the room. Daniel looked around himself again. "I am a stupid man. I am waiting for people… But nobody could come into the room because there aren't any door here," Daniel thought.

"There is a unique exit through the blue window. Perhaps I should have learned how to fly before I found myself in this room." He smiled.

"I could stay in the room for a long time but I do not like the black color of the ceiling. It brings dark emotions into my heart. I should do something because it is beginning to irritate me. Maybe I should fall asleep again... So, I will wake up in my real life. Perhaps I stay in my night dream. I read similar stories about people who woke up in their dreams."

He closed his eyes. "This darkness reminds me of the black color of the ceiling of this room," he smiled.

Daniel waited for some minutes and opened his eyes. "It could be a strange thing if I found myself in another place now. My closed eyes were like the closed window of this room. The doors of my dream were not opened to me and I could not leave this room. Perhaps I have the only way to leave this place. It is the blue window."

Daniel came to the window again. He opened the window with shout of surprise. A little yellow bird was sitting on the windowsill and looking at Daniel with interest. Daniel climbed on the windowsill and sat down near the bird.

"Who are you?" He asked.

He was not expecting any answer. He wanted to calm himself with this question. The yellow bird flew away into the white space of emptiness.

"I am a lone man again." Daniel thought ironically.

"Perhaps I should not ask the bird any question. So the bird would become my friend in this horror place of white stillness."

Daniel looked around. The white space had some changes. Some colors were added to its stillness. Also he began to hear different voices. There were voices of men and women. Tender voices of the beautiful children sounded like little bells in surrounding space.

"People live here too. I do not see them but I hear

their voices. They talk with each other. Children's laughter mixes with voices of adults." He thought.

Daniel stood up on the windowsill and cried to them, "I am here! Please, come to me. I am feeling very lonely here. I do not see you but you are not far from me because I can hear your voices."

Nothing changed. The talks were like a music of the sea waves. He heard them but people did not.

"Crazy place," Daniel was indignant at this situation. "And... What should I do? I cannot sleep. I hear the talks but people do not notice my call to them."

He sat down on the windowsill and began to swing his legs in the white space. "I will shake up this white space and the space will let me go," Daniel joked to himself. He stopped being angry and began to sing his favorite song.

The same yellow bird appeared from the white space and sat down on the windowsill near Daniel again.

"I am a great singer! The birds fly to me because they want to listen to my song. We will sing together if this bird learns the words of my song."

Daniel laughed. He had always been a light-hearted person.

Other yellow birds appeared from the white emptiness.

"Wow! I will organize a chorus of birds. And I will be the main singer in this chorus."

Daniel laughed again.

The space was full of the different voices and many yellow birds.

Suddenly a tender voice asked him to open his eyes.

"How I may open my eyes if they are already opened?"

He was surprised.

The voice was not similar to the other voices of the white space.

"I must recollect this voice," Daniel thought. "Yes, it is Jenny's voice. My beautiful wife... The happiness of my life..." Daniel recollected. "She would not ask me to open my eyes if it was a stupid idea. So, I should try to do it."

And Daniel opened his eyes.

Jenny was sitting near him on his bed. Her beautiful eyes were full of tears.

"Who offended you?" Daniel asked her, "I will kill any person who dared to offend you!"

"My darling... My Daniel... You were so close to death because of your illness. I thought that you could leave me. I am so happy that you opened your eyes. You are talking to me ..."

Jenny burst into tears. And Daniel recollected what happened. He wanted to tell Jenny about the strange white space which he had visited.

He wanted to tell her about voices of people that he had heard in this space.

Daniel remembered the strange colored room with its black ceiling and the blue window where he had met his friend the bird.

But Jenny did not allow him to tell anything, "My dear... Please, do not talk. You should be quiet. Doctor told me that I must care about it."

Several weeks passed away and Daniel was in good health again. Daniel forgot about the white space and other things that had happened during his illness. Jenny was happy. She supposed that his stories were due to hallucinations because of Daniel's fever.

Only one thing amazed Daniel. He often saw a beautiful yellow bird in his garden. Jenny and Daniel had never seen that bird before his illness. Daniel did not understand the reason but the song of that bird always made him happy.

The secret of feelings

Harry and Emily were in love. They were a beautiful couple. Their friends could not discover the secret of their beautiful relations. They had lived together many happy years. Their friends had experienced many changes during that period. But Harry and Emily lived inside a world of happy life. Harry cared about Emily. Emily thought only about Harry. She was glad about every flower which Harry brought to her.

He liked to see that gladness in her beautiful blue eyes. They often talked with each other. They were together in the evenings.

They opened the windows to the bright sunshine in the mornings.

Many friends were very curious about a secret of their love. Their friends wanted to know this secret too. "Maybe we could be a happy because of this secret."

They thought from time to time. Emily kept silence. She never told anybody about the relations with her husband. But Harry decided to help their friends to become happier. Therefore, he invited friends in an open-air cafe for talking about Emily. The friends had many questions. They could not understand what Harry valued in such an ordinary woman as Emily was in their opinion. "Emily is not a very beautiful woman. She is not a very clever woman because she graduated only from school. We know that she could not pass the examinations for the Institute. She likes flowers, but it is a usual thing for many women," they told Harry.

Harry laughed, "She is so beautiful at the moment I am offering flowers to her. She is like a little sun for me at that moment. Do you know that Emily prepares a beautiful surprise for me every day?"

"Now I will describe those wonderful surprises," he continued. Harry retold stories that Emily had entrusted to him. There were stories about her childhood and school years. There were stories about her dreams and hopes. He wanted his friends to understand that Emily was a rare wonderful woman.

"Yes. You are right. She is really a very interesting woman," his friends told him at last, "We must drink a good wine for it!" Harry was proud that he was able to convince of the friends.

Later the friends asked Harry about Emily again. They told Harry that he was helping them with it. And Harry told his friends about love, Emily's feelings, his trust, their hopes and dreams. Harry was sure that he knew all things about it. It was a usual evening. Harry came back to the flat after a hard long day of work.

He looked at Emily who was smiling to him by her usual tender smile. "She is not a very beautiful woman.

My friends were right." Harry thought sadly.

Emily was showing him the vase with flowers that she had placed on the table in the kitchen. "I put very different flowers in one vase. I have such an interesting result! Please, Harry, have a look! It is like a painting," she burst out laughing.

"She is not a very clever woman. My friends were right," Harry thought.

Emily began to tell him about the little events that had happened during that day. "Her stories are boring stories. She is a really stupid woman. My clever friends were right, as always they were."

"You were right. My feeling to Emily was not true love. It was only an illusion. I understood that I should find a new woman. I am cleverer than Emily is. I am more beautiful than she is. She is too ordinary woman," Harry complained to the friends when they were drinking coffee in the same open-air cafe.

His friends were glad to hear it. They did not want to admit to themselves that they were glad to hear it.

But it was so.

They thought, "The secret of feelings... It is funny!

Our friend Harry is a very clever person. However, he also did not discover the secret of love."

Green lake

"It is a strange place," Robert thought. "I have never visited so unusual places before."

He was walking in a big forest of colored trees. He remembered that he began his walk in the usual forest which was not far from his house. He often walked along the narrow paths of that forest. On that day he was going along the old path when he saw that the trunks of the trees were changing to unusual colors. Every tree had a new color that was different from the previous tree. Robert understood that he did not know the names of many colors because they were very different from usual colors. There were many birds on the trees. But they were similar to each other in size and by their green color. They were on the branches of the trees like numerous green leaves.

Robert looked at the sky and he realized that the sky became the window to another world. He saw people in the sky. Robert saw buses and cars.

"Strange place…" Robert thought. "People are walking on the glass of the sky."

He thought, "A road to another world…"

Robert looked around him carefully. There were many bright little flowers everywhere on the ground. He wanted to pick up one of them but he could not do it. The flowers were like an essential piece of the ground. A beautiful music was flying around him like a fresh wind.

"If somebody asks me about this strange place where I am now, then I will not have enough words to describe it," Robert thought.

The rain came from the big sky-window. It was an instantaneous change in the appearance of the forest. At that moment the colored trees changed their colors to the usual color of trees. The birds-leaves flew away in the sky-window. The forest was in a sad rainy mood. Only the soft music sounded.

"The changes of the weather remind me changes of mood of my beloved woman," Robert laughed. "It is not easy to understand her. She stays in a good mood. Suddenly she may become sad like this gray day. Often I do not understand her emotions. Perhaps this strange place is like her soul which is so far from my understanding." The rain stopped after some minutes.

"I did not notice that the ground became wet with this rain. I do not see any drops on the flowers either," Robert thought. "Oh! I can see a bright green lake… Perhaps green fish abound in the lake." He smiled at his joke and went to the lake. It was a small green lake with a big yellow flower at the center. The view of the untroubled surface of the lake brought serenity to Robert's heart.

He began to think about it all reasonably.

"The lake maybe in the forest although the color of the water is a strange bright green color. I see the transparent sky-window with people in it. It is a strange sky. Soft music is flying around me like a fresh wind. It is not usual for the forest either. I can draw the conclusion that I understand nothing," he decided after his reflections about the situation.

He came to the lake and looked at the water. Nothing. Of course, he waited to see a reflection of his face. But the reflection did not exist on the green water of that lake. Then he put his hand inside the water. Robert imagined that a little red crocodile would look at him from the water. But it is not happened.

"Crocodiles do not live here," he joked.

It was the usual cold water of the lake. Robert sat down on the grass by the water, "I need some rest before I go further. Maybe it is unsafe to proceed further. I have seen so many unusual illogical things here that it is too much for me."

Robert lay on the grass and began to look at the sky-window.

"Wow! It is better than my TV-set at home," he thought. "The life of the unknown world in the sky. I can see people who are walking behind the glass of the sky. They are talking with each other. I can see a wonderful red sun and yellow clouds above those people too. It is the sky for those people."

Robert sat down and took some water from the lake in his hands. At that moment he gave a shout because something was written with white words upon the green water.

"Nobody understands where words come from," he read.

The water leaked out through his fingers and his palms became empty. Robert took the water in his palms again. New white phrases were written on the green page of the water.

"Do not try to analyze the country of poetry.

NEVER."

The water returned to the green lake between his fingers. His palms were empty again.

"I never wrote poems," Robert thought. "Why am I in such a strange place and read this strange message of the green lake?"

He scooped up some water again. The white message was very short.

"Love her without hesitation."

"My beloved woman is the only woman for me. I do not understand her emotions sometimes but

I love her." He thought.

"Why was this message written for me? She often writes poems. I like many of them. I always want to know where she takes her beautiful words. Her world is so…," Robert stopped.

He thought that he discovered the meaning of the phrases.

"I can not understand something of her emotional world. But the place where I am now is a very strange place. I do not understand it either. Maybe I cannot imagine where she "walks" when she writes her poems. But it is not important if something is not obvious."

Nobody understands where words come from.

Do not try to analyze poetry.

Love her without hesitation.

Robert wanted to read the next message. But the water remained the usual water without any words written upon it.

"I think I understand the meaning correctly. Perhaps I had only three attempts to read it. It can not be repeated if I did not understand it clearly."

Robert looked around him. He was in the usual forest. The sky was a wonderful blue sky with white clouds. Robert knew many paths through the forest going to his house. He was happy. His beloved woman waited for him. Robert was sure that she was reading a book in the garden. She liked to be there in the warm evenings.

Unuseful Words

"I have written your name in the sky. Have you seen my words written with white clouds? I have given my songs to the birds. Have you heard these songs in the early morning? I have told my words to the fresh wind. Have you felt a kiss of the wind on your cheek on a hot summer day?"

Ian stopped writing a story. He looked at the door. He was constantly waiting for Luci to open the door. His room could be full of her laughter again. He remembered Luci was always ready to laugh. Ian did not like it. He thought that it was something belonging to the space of stupid thoughts. Ian used to look at her very strictly. So, Luci felt confused under his look and turned grave.

"You should not laugh so often!" He told Luci.

Ian's idea was that an adult woman must be quiet and serious.

"It will gain the respect of other people to you," he told her at those moments. Luci agreed. She loved Ian and trusted his clever words.

She liked to bring flowers into their room that she picked up in the green field. But there were uninteresting flowers in Ian's opinion.

"I will buy the beautiful rich bouquets for you if you want to have the bouquets in the room," he told her. "It is most unsuitable to put such unattractive flowers in our room."

Luci agreed. And she did not bring flowers anymore in the home after Ian got very angry when she placed them in a vase again.

Ian often brought to her bright bouquets. But she took them without joy. Luci did not tell him that the field flowers reminded her of her childhood.

She was not sure that Ian could understand what did she mean.

Ian recollected that Luci liked the opened windows of their home at nighttime. She frequently sat down on a windowsill and looked at the night sky.

"What do you see there?" Ian asked her irritatedly.

"I can not explain it, my love." Luci answered tenderly. "But I really need it. It is such a beautiful tale for me!"

Ian used to close the windows. "My dear, it is a stupid idea to sit on the window-sill and look at the empty sky. You might catch a cold. The air is too fresh now. Many moths fly into the room through the opened windows. We will have a problem to sleep because of it."

"You are right, my dear," Luci replied to him sadly.

She used to bring a cup of strong coffee to Ian because he thought that a coffee would help him to understand the books properly. Ian read the only useful books. He did not like poems. Ian was always angry if he saw a book of the poems in her hands.

"You waste your time, my dear," Ian told Luci.

She put the book back on the shelf. Luci did not like quarrels.

"Every quarrel destroys a piece of my soul," Luci tried to explain it.

"A piece of my soul..." Ian thought. "I do not understand why she likes to use so words. I think she should say simpler phrase like this "I do not like to have a quarrel. It is enough for describing a situation."

Ian looked at the door again.

"Seven years have passed since I met Luci," he thought. "And I cannot find her now. She told me she had died some time ago. It was such a strange talk. I remember all of her words but I did not understand what she wanted to tell me that day."

"I have written your name in the sky. Have you seen my words written with white clouds? I have given my song to the birds. Have you heard these songs in the early morning? I have told my words to the fresh wind. Have you felt a kiss of the wind on your cheek on a hot summer day?"

The woman came to his table and put the cup of strong coffee on it.

"Thank you, my dear Luci," he told her. "Please,

read these words. I have written them to you. Do you remember how you liked to sit down on the window-sill at night-time?"

Luci read the words and said, "Perhaps they are beautiful words if you like them, my dear husband."

She kissed him.

"I have brought you a cup of coffee. I am sorry, I am a bit tired today. I am going to sleep. Please, do not open the windows because moths would fly into our room."

Every day is a little life

"My mother told me that every day is a little life. I remember this talk. She was a very clever woman. I was a child at that time," Robert was saying to his little son Henry.

"It is funny that I should be saying the same words to you now. I cannot believe that I became so adult that I have got a son. I lost many true emotions because I did not trust the words of my mother. She told me that I must use every day with careful attention because I live in it.

It is a wonderful thing that one day is separated from another day by a long night. So we have a possibility to understand that our full life is not so long as we think. Every little step is a step on a long way but it must be done if we want to enter another day. Every little step is like a brick for a big building which we build every day. Our building… Our life…"

Robert looked at his son and smiled. Henry did not listen to his words with attention. He was thinking about a big fish which he wanted to catch in a beautiful lake. That lake was situated not far from their house. Every day Henry and his friends ran to the lake which was a huge world of different emotions for the boys. He did not think about the long way of his life. It was so uninteresting for him. But Henry loved his father. Therefore, he was sitting on the sofa near him.

"Poor father," the boy was thinking. "Every day is a little life. Our life is like a big building which we create by ourselves… I think it would be a more interesting time for my father if we could go to the lake together. Father has not been at the lake for several months. He goes to work every day except Sundays. He watches TV movies on Sundays. Is it his little life? Poor father.... The sun and clouds are so beautiful above the lake. The water is fresh and colorful. Does he remember that the water of the lake has various colors because of the rays of the sun? Does he remember how looks the green grass? I am not sure."

The father was continuing his serious talk with his son, "You should choose a job. Every day you should make something important at your job for your future success because every day is your little life."

Robert looked at Henry, "My dear son, I told you important words. Please, save them in your mind."

"I will remember your words, my dear father! May I go to the lake now?" Henry asked with a happy smile because at last such a long talk was finished.

"Yes, my dear, you may do it. Please, do not come home too late." The father told his son. Then he began to watch a movie about World War III. He liked such kind of movies because he thought that they made him a more clever person.

Henry called his friends and they ran to the lake. It was a beautiful space of nature that always offered many wonderful things for children. The trees played soft melodies with green leaves. The clouds were so different that the boys liked to imagine the painted animals on them. The grass was like a green carpet. They sat down on the bank of the beautiful lake and began to catch fish. The weather was calm. So, the lake was like the strange mirror of another world with the reflections of the trees and the moving clouds on it.

"But the fish live inside the mirror too!" Henry burst out laughing.

He and his friends were sitting without talking and were looking at the water of the lake. The birds sang their sunny songs. Butterflies were flying above wonderful flowers. Little ants ran along the boys' feet. The boys were sitting and looking at the water.

"We have become a piece of nature," Henry thought. "I am like the tree now because I am alive and motionless. I have feelings though I am motionless. I would like that the trees could tell me about their feelings."

The day was a hot summer day. Therefore, the boys stopped fishing and decided to swim in the fresh lake. "We are going inside the mirror! We are like the clouds! We will swim among the clouds in the lake!" Henry cried to his friends.

"Now I am like a big fish. I think the other fishes are very surprised at my size," Henry thought with pride. "It is strange to think that I am a little boy for adults but such a big fish for the other fishes in this lake."

Later he and his friends were sitting on the bank with serious faces again. "Now we are the great anglers again. It is not important if we would not catch any fish. Present fishing is wonderful." Henry thought. "Poor father... He goes to work every day. He makes little steps to his success every day. He told me that every day should be like a little life. Does he like his everyday life? Father told me that I must make something important every day for my future success. Perhaps I waste my time now." Henry became sad. He really loved his father and trusted him.

"Perhaps I am a stupid boy."

He looked around him. The birds sang a beautiful evening song. The color of the leaves of the trees was changed to a deep green color because of the sunset. The mirror of the lake was showing the reflections of the boys who were sitting on the green grass. Sometimes a fresh wind touched the water of the lake. Then the reflections of the boys, the trees and the white clouds were dancing because of the moving water.

"Every day is a little life... I like this day. I am full of emotions. I know that I will recollect these summer days during cold winter. I did not do something significant today. I did not do something for my future success. But I was honest with myself," Henry thought.

He was not sure that his father was right.

"I think I became a better boy today because all deep emotions of nature were kept in my heart. Today I became stronger because of my feelings. Therefore, my "little life" was wonderful," the boy smiled. And he did not realize that he was like the great philosopher at that moment.

The story about a painter

"It is very easy to make happy life," a painter thought one usual morning. "I can't change the world. I can't change most of the situations I do not like. But I can create a little world of happiness for me."

The painter came in his flat. He did not wait for any special time for creating his "new world". He was calm and sure. He did not tell anybody about his decision.

For many months he painted the walls of his little flat, the floor and the ceiling. He painted new windows and flowers and many beautiful images that I will not describe because it was a secret spiritual world of the painter. One day "the artwork" was finished. It was the painter's emotional world that had become a visible world.

"I am the great painter," he thought. "I may stay in this painted world all the time."

But he had to leave the flat every day. It was important for him to get some money. The painter created portraits for people who asked him to do it. He worked in the street. In the evenings he came back in his flat.

The painter wanted to be happy. And it was so when he opened the door of his beautiful painted flat. The flat was saving his hopes and gladness. The flat was like a true friend for him.

The painter decided to invite his friends in his flat too.

"I should show my painted flat. My friends will have many deep emotions with it. They will praise me." The painter thought.

The next day his friends were invited to visit his flat. They had wanted to do it because it was interesting for them to see the new great artwork of the painter. The painter opened the door of his flat. The friends came in carefully.

"Why did you use so bright colors?" They asked him.

"That was a stupid idea to paint new windows on the walls. You have real windows! Did you forget about them?" They laughed at him. "Why did you paint flowers on the floors? It maybe a good idea for a woman's flat."

Many similar words were said to the painter.

He was standing in the middle of the room while his friends were traveling in his emotional world because of the flat. They did not wish to offend the painter. They sincerely did not understand the painter's ideas. His friends were really surprised with his funny painted flat.

The painter brought the bottles of a wonderful old wine he had bought for that meeting specially.

He had dreamed that he would open the bottles at the end of the meeting when the delighted voices of his friends would have sounded like a beautiful music for him.

His surprised friends left his flat. The painter went into the kitchen. He took a glass of the wine in his hand and cried. He would never be able to love the world of his beautiful flat anymore. He looked sadly at the funny bright flowers that he had painted on the floor of the kitchen. They were like real flowers that had been trampled by his friends.

The town of crazy people

"I would like to tell people only the truth," a little boy told his mother. "I don't want to lie."

"It is a good decision," a mother answered. "But you should remember that you might have to live in a special unique town in the world known as "The town of crazy people". I do not believe that they are really crazy people. I think people of other towns imagine them like crazy people. We can go to the town. Then it will be easy for you to make a final decision, my dear boy."

The next day they woke up early in the morning. The mother put on her best clothes. She gave her hand to her son, and they went along the bank of the river to the town of honest people. It was a long way. It took them several days before the town could be seen in the distance. The mother and the son came to the gate which was the only entrance to the town. "No entry." The words were written on the old gate. The boy was perplexed.

"How could I visit the town if so words are written on the gate?" He asked his mother.

The mother did not know it, "I suppose we should wait here until somebody comes to the gate. Maybe this person will ask us about a goal of our visit."

They sat down on the grass and began to wait for someone from the town. About an hour later a tall man opened the gate.

"Oh! I am sorry. I did not know you had been waiting for me!" The man told them.

"What can I do for you, my dear travellers?" He asked with a kind smile.

"My son wants to live among honest people. He dreams to be with people who never lie," the mother answered.

The man became very serious.

"Poor boy ... or... Happy boy... I do not know. He is late. The town has kept the same title "The town of crazy people". The same people live in the town except one person who left the town many years ago. But it is not the town of honest people anymore. Do you know how difficult it is to tell the truth to each other? One example only... My friend asked my opinion about a woman who was the most beautiful woman for him. He loved her. What should I tell him? The truth... In my opinion she was a stupid woman. Yes. She was really pretty but I had no high opinion about her mind. Of course, I did not tell him the truth. They married. Now they are a happy family. Was my truth reality? I do not know. I could lose the right to live in this town if I told somebody that I lied to my friend. Therefore, I did not tell anybody about it. For many years people of "crazy town" had been proud to stay honest. They did not care what impression they made. "Crazy town of crazy people"... Do you know that a lie changes your life? It is really so. A lie is a strange thing. I think it may change a soul. It is like a weed that grows among flowers. So... People of the town began to realize that most of them did not express their real thoughts. Situations were like this one I described before. People did not want to offend each other. They wanted to stay friends. One person left the town at the beginning of that process. He was one of my friends. I asked him to take me with him. But he told me that he would live in a little house which was built in a lone place, "The only nature does not lie. Loneliness is a simple way to understand a language of nature. I want to listen to the talks of white clouds. I want to listen to the songs of beautiful birds. I want to fly by the night sky. I hope my dreams will be the world of truth for me. But I need to stay alone. Otherwise, I will not hear much important truth." There were the words of my friend. He had written the words "No entry" on the gate of the town before he left the town. He did not believe in the light future of the town. The people of the town knew about the words on the gate. Therefore, they did not expect any new persons in the town. I was really surprised that you, my beautiful guests, waited for me before the gate."

The man smiled to the mother and her son. The boy became very sad. The man noticed it. He tried to comfort the young boy. "It is very hard to live among honest people. You are young. You will be changed with time. Sometimes you'd better not tell the truth if you want to save your spiritual world. Opened spiritual world is like the field where people can collect flowers but it is not good for you."

"So, please, tell me. Do you want to come into the town?" The man asked the boy.

"Oh! No. I don't." The boy answered.

The man looked at him attentively. Then he told the boy sadly, "You see… You have lied me. I know it because I heard many lies in my life."

The boy was confused.

"So… Now you may understand perfectly what I told you. You did not want to offend me. You wanted to be polite. The lie is flying above our heads because of your answer. It was really the unique town of crazy people because only crazy people can always tell the truth to each other.

Now they are ordinary people. I am an ordinary man too. Perhaps I have lost something important in my life. Unfortunately I did not realize what it was for me. You are a wonderful boy. I am sure that your life will be beautiful. And... I hope my friend who had left the town did not regret being honest.

A strange meeting

It was a strange meeting. It happened one day I was at home. A rainy day… I listened to the music of the sad rain. Music came to my home with the drops of rain.

Suddenly someone rang my doorbell. It was a young girl who was standing there and looking at me.

"May I come in?" She asked. "I will be glad," I answered.

She sat down by the table in the kitchen. She did not say anything. She listened to the words of the rain. I was surprised. Nevertheless, I kept silent too. She was so young and beautiful. Her eyes reminded me of the blue sky on sunny days. Her dress was yellow. She looked like a strange yellow flower. It was so interesting that I began to ask her questions. They were simple questions about life. Her replies were clever and strong. Then I began to ask about serious things that had always interested me. Dreams, death, love …

"What do you think about it?" I asked the strange girl.

She gave me answers without any hesitation. Her thoughts were very clever. I could not understand how I felt about her words. It was something more than I could express with words. She was looking at me with a tender smile.

Rain… Evening opened its eyes and the streets became darker. I offered hot tea to my little guest. Suddenly I heard a new ring at my door.

"Strange day..." I thought.

A beautiful woman was standing behind the door.

"Come in," I told her.

She went into my kitchen. She did not say "good evening" to the girl. She sat down near her as if she was alone with me in the kitchen. Rain was playing its music.

I was confused. I did not understand what was happening. It began to be intriguing for me.

I began to talk with the woman. She was also beautiful. The woman was calm and sad. Our talk was very interesting for me too. She told me important things that I had always liked to know. Fate, friendship, creativity, eternity… She knew much about it. However, she had many hesitations. She told me that she was not sure that she was right. She asked me to open the window so that we could listen fully to the music of the rain.

The joyful girl and sad woman were sitting with me in the kitchen. Who were they? I did not know. I knew that they were cleverer, stronger and more beautiful than I was on the day of our meeting. I had received the answers to the questions that were important for me. The tender music of the rain was playing in my city. The window was open. I turned away for a minute to make a cup of tea for the woman too. The kitchen was empty when I looked at the table. The rain had stopped. The silence deepened. I had the impression that both the woman and the girl had gone with the rain which had played music with its drops. The window was closed.

"They went through the open window," I thought.

I forgot all the clever words which had been told me by the woman and the girl. I had troubles and reflection in my mind again.

And I understood… The girl and the woman was me. The girl came to me from my childhood. I recalled that wonderful yellow dress which was my favorite dress when I was a young girl. I recalled my sad thoughts that were told me by the woman. If I lose something important from my spiritual world then I may have another strange meeting with the girl and other new women in the future. One of them will be what I am now.

And I will not recognize her. Her thoughts and wishes will be unusual and strange for me. They will come to me with the cold rain and go with the fresh wind through my open window.

A strange meeting on the road of my life...

Three worlds

Nicholas lived in a beautiful town. He liked to walk along canals of the town. The air was full of the breath of the sea. He had read that the town was built on many islands. It was a city of bridges and rivers. They were so different that Nicholas gave new names to them. The names were not the same as their official names. He liked to think about them with new titles. Nicholas gave new names to the long streets and palaces. Great palaces were built in many parts of the town. It was both a real and an unreal town for Nicholas because he mixed his own spiritual world with the transparent spiritual world of the town. Nicholas liked different places in the town. For example, he liked to walk in a little park of much stillness and beauty. The park was like a true friend for him. Nicholas knew every small road in the park. He listened to the old trees' talks. He imagined that he understood their wise green words. There was a small bench near the oldest tree. Sometimes the bench was taken by another person who came in the park too. It was as if somebody came into his emotional world without permission.

Another beautiful world was a world of his dreams. It was the lovely town of his childhood. It was a town of his recollections. It was possible to be there with his night dreams. He awaited for the meeting with that town during his daily life. That town was very different from the present town. There were not many bridges, palaces and parks. The only old brown bridge was built across the single river of the town.

And a small white church was built on the hill. It was the town of his happy childhood days. He often met his parents in his night dreams. It was usually so. He entered the room. His father and mother hugged him. Then they sat down at the table and his mother brought the cups with tasty black tea to them. Nicholas liked his beautiful old cup. The colorful town was painted on the cup. It was the usual evening of his childhood. His mother and father died many years ago. The same cup of his childhood stood on the real table in his apartment in the real town. Every morning he was glad that, by chance, he had not broken the cup. Usual life of dishes is not very long. He took the cup in his hands.

"It is the unique town among my three towns that I can take in my hands. It is a fairy town that is painted on the cup. I like this nice guest from my childhood," Nicholas thought happily.

So… Nicholas was a rich person because he had three wonderful towns. They were the real one where he lived, the town of his childhood in his dreams and the nice town painted on the cup. It was his secret world. He never told anybody about it.

One day in the Spring, he met a young joyful girl. She was so pretty that he fell in love with her. She reminded him of a butterfly.

"She is a piece of the Spring. She has come from the space of tenderness. I can trust her." Nicholas thought.

He showed his favorite places of the town to the girl. He told her about the secret names that he had given them. He told her about his night dreams in which he had a meeting with his mother and father. At last Nicholas told her the story of the old cup with the beautiful fairy town painted on it. He wanted to make the girl a piece of his beautiful worlds.

Several months later, the girl got very angry with him. He could not remember a reason of quarrel. It was a stupid quarrel because of a trifle. But he remembered all the rough words that she said to him. The girl told him that she was very tired of his stupid fantasies. She told many other terrible words. Nicholas did not want to recollect them after the quarrel, but they were flying in the kitchen although the girl had left Nicholas after the quarrel.

Nicholas was standing in the kitchen among flying rough words around him. He had never felt such a huge loneliness. The girl had thrown his old cup onto the floor with anger before she left his apartment. The town, which was the heart of the cup, has been broken into many small pieces. So, his beautiful old cup was dead.

Nicholas sat down on the chair in the middle of the kitchen. He thought about his real town. Would it possible for him to love it again? He thought about a meeting with his mother and father in his dreams. He was not sure that new meetings would happen. Nicholas took three pieces of his beautiful cup. He thought that it was like he was holding three broken towns in his hands.

New music of the rain

The rain came into the city. People had been waiting for the rain for several months but the rain had its own life that did not depend on people's wishes. It was a usual summer day.

But it was not a usual city because it was the city of painters. Yes, it was a strange city where only painters lived. They were friendly to each other. They did not envy anyone because every painter was a talented person. Every painter was afraid to lose the talent which he had. They had read an old book regarding art that talent could leave the painters. It could happen if envy became their hearts' mistress.

Nobody wanted such a destiny. Therefore, it was a fantastic city of the talented people.

The rain was a very young rain that had never visited the city before. It came into every garden of the city. It came in every house. There were many beautiful artworks in the houses of the painters. The melodies sounded with every wonderful painting. So, the music of the rain were colored with new emotions. They were the emotions of hopes, gladness and dreams.

"I have never seen so strange people."

The rain decided, "I should share these melodies to other cities with help of my fresh drops."

The rain left the city a few days later. It was not the same cold gray rain that had come into the city because its soul was full of wonderful melodies and colors. The citizens of other cities were very surprised with new music of the rain. They were opening the windows of their house for listening beautiful music.

"The rain healed my sadness while beautiful melodies sounded in the wet streets," people said to each other after the rain. "It was a very strange rain of colorful emotions. We remember that previous rains brought other feelings. It was a sad feeling of night sky. It was a sad feeling of cold winds. The present rain is like the smile of a happy day."

The rain was proud of the people's warm words in different cities. It flew to new cities that people could listen to the simple beautiful melodies which the rain had taken from the city of the painters.

One day the rain met its own friends. Surely they were the rains too. The rain told them about the strange city where kindness and talent have been in every house. The rains decided to find the city again that the friends could take the melodies of the paintings too. They tried to find the city for many months. However, they did not find it.

Maybe the envy had come into the hearts of the painters and the city was changed to a usual city. Maybe it was not easy to find the city of happy painters. The rains did not know the answer. Therefore, the only one young rain kept in its soul the melodies of the paintings. Always people recognize beauty of its music.

They tell each other whenever the young rain comes into their city, "Please, listen to the beautiful music of the drops. It is that rain of colorful music that healing and bring a hope.

A smile

A smile was a little boy's precious gift while he was walking with his mother in the rainy city.

His mother was thinking about the different problems of her life. She did not like the gray color of that day. It was a spring day but the weather was not kind to people. High sky was full of gray clouds. They closed the sun's eyes. The sun did not want to have a look at angry people. Only a little boy did not think about bad weather and the gray color of the day. He was happy because his mother had bought a red toy car to him. The boy was running with his red car along the street. He imagined that he became a great driver. Suddenly the boy noticed a wonderful color butterfly. He stopped and his laughter sounded like a little bell.

The boy looked at his mother and shouted to her, "Mum! Have a look! It is the same butterfly which I met last summer. I have recognized it… This butterfly has the same eyes and the same color of wings. I think the butterfly is my friend because I used to meet it in different places where we walked together, my Mum. Therefore, this butterfly is my friend!"

The boy burst out laughing again. The mother looked at her little son and her face was kissed by his gladness. She forgot about her problems. The mother was full of the sunny gladness by her son.

She thought, "My son … My son is my little sun."

"Yes. It is the same butterfly," she told seriously to her son. "You are right. The butterfly is your friend because it flew to you from last summer."

The mother took a little hand of her son. He waved farewell to the butterfly. The mother and the son went along the street again. The mother was smiling to the funny thoughts of her little son. She looked at the man who was walking next to her. The man was surprised with the smile of the unknown beautiful woman. The man smiled to her too. He was very proud that such a beautiful woman had a look at him. The mother and the son were walking along the street. They had a talk about very serious things that are so important for children like flowers, butterflies and toys.

The inspired man came in his home. He kissed his old mother. The mother became a happy woman because of his care. The received smile made happy a new person again. Many people met the little boy and her mother in the street. Everyone smiled to the little joyful boy. His smile was like the color butterfly which he called like "my friend". The smile was flying from one person to another. The sun liked kind people. It opened the eyes and removed all gray clouds from the sky. The sunny day was made by the simple smile of the little boy.

The boy did not realize it. He was going on his happy usual walk with his beautiful mother.

Heaven bless this house

"You are like a closed window if you do not believe it," the old man told Rod. "You cannot hear it or see it if you are in such a state of mind".

The young boy became sad, "My mother died some months ago. I do not know how I will live without her."

He cried. The old man took his little hand in his hand, "How sure are you that your mother does not see you now? How can you be so sure that life does not exist after the death?"

He stroked his head.

"Do you remember how you lived in your mother's womb?" The old man asked the boy.

"No," the boy answered quietly.

"But you lived there for nine long months. You had different emotions. You heard the voices of people. You listened to sounds of real life which were far from you at that time."

"I do not remember how I was born by my mother either," Rod told the old man.

"Yes. It was the birth. But it was like death for you, my dear little friend. You were leaving a world of small space that was only your space by your beautiful mother. Therefore, we cannot be sure that death is the end of being for people. It can be a new birth too."

"Why hasn't anybody come back to us and tell us about it?" The boy asked with tears.

"How could it be, my dear? Could you return to the first days of your birth? Time cannot be turned back. And... Could you be returned to the womb of your mother if you wished it? Maybe the space of our present world is highly small for people who left this world too. They cannot come back into this space even if they wish to do it. I hope that they can fly."

The old man looked at the night sky sadly. He contemplated the past. His arm went around the child. Rod moved close to the old man.

It was a serious long talk. The high night sky was looking at the two lone figures that were sitting on the old bench in the calm huge garden.

"Maybe the people who left this world have an unusual possibility to talk with us, but we cannot understand their language," the old man told the boy.

"Perhaps the unique possibility of a usual talk with us is the talk through dreams of people. But people forget it all when they open their eyes in the morning. And... If they remember something, then they do not want to believe it." The old man smiled sadly.

"I think my mother is alive in a space which is unknown space to me now. But I cannot see my mother. It is so sad... I cannot kiss her." Rod told his old wise friend.

"Yes. It is so," the old man answered. "But you cannot see the wind either although it exists. You cannot see aroma of flowers but it is a reality. You cannot see my words, but they become the reality when I tell them to you."

"But I see the wind because of the moving of clouds in the sky. I see the wind with the cold air that embraces my body. I see the wind with the moving of grass and the leaves of the trees in the garden," the boy told the old man.

"My dear philosopher," the old man answered Rod with a serious expression in his eyes, "You answered to the question by yourself. You have found clever words. Although you did not realize the depth of the words which you have just told me now," the old man resumed.

"It was an idea that I wanted to explain to you with my previous words about the closed window. But you, my little philosopher, have found clearer words to explain it." The old man smiled to him.

"We can not see many important things but it does not mean that they do not exist if they are not visible for people. You are right that we can recognize these things through indirect results that we can see such as the moving of grass, for example.

Perhaps the people who left this world give a sign to us from time to time but busy people of our world are so careless to any signs. Also they do not trust dream. Maybe it is a right way that people could be more earthbound. Maybe it is a mistake of people. So, they lose something important. I do not know."

The boy sighed. "Sometimes I see my mother in my dreams. She is so joyful there. She is like a young girl."

"Yes. Your mother will be near you during your long life. I am sure that beloved people are near us even though they have left this world," the old man told Rod. A light rain kissed the cheeks of the boy at that moment.

"It is like a tender kiss by my mother." The boy smiled and looked at the sky.

The old man took the hand of the boy in his big warm hand.

"We should go inside the house. The rain will be heavier soon. I think it would not be right to tell something more now. I am sure that you understand me, my dear boy. You have a tender soul and a strong mind."

They went to the brightly lit opened door of the house. Some minutes later they closed the door. A little while after, the rain stopped.

The deep stillness of the garden was full of the beautiful emotions by the calm night sky.

Colored Silhouettes

Nick was a person who never thought about the meaning of life. Every day was a usual day for him. Nick had closed the door to the part of his memory where his recollections lived.

"I am glad that I am alive. I can have a glass of good wine every day. I have an interesting job. It is enough for me."

He was 30 years old. One usual evening he was sitting in front of his TV-set. The movie was so boring that Nick fell asleep. It often happened when Nick watched movies. The glass of the red wine was on the table as usual.

Nick entered into a colored dream. It was as if somebody opened the door to the room in his memory where his recollections had lived for many long years. The recollections reminded him of funny children playing games. They laughed and jumped. They were really like real children because the recollections had their own wishes and goals. Sometimes they left Nick to visit the places where they were born.

So... A strange connection existed between Nick's soul and the recollections. When the door of the memory was opened, then some of his recollections flew to Nick's soul. The color of his soul was dull and gray. The recollections did not find any bright beautiful colors in it.

"Oh! It is not a light place," they told each other. "We should help Nick."

They jumped inside the gray sea of his soul.

Many little lights appeared inside that sea with the recollections. A strange wonderful music sounded in the sea of his soul. At the same moment Nick went into the village of his childhood in his dream. He realized the fact that he was in the dream-world because it was too strange a world for real life. The village looked empty. The doors of all the small houses were closed. Many colored birds were flying above Nick. The flowers were huge. They were as high as the trees. But the trees did not exist in the village. Nick turned up his head to the sky. The sky was a blue tender color but the sun did not look at Nick from the sky. There were only many little suns hanging above all small houses that stood along the street of the village.

"I am sleeping. It can not be real life," Nick thought. "It is like decorations in a theatre. Where are the actors?" He smiled. "I can wake up now. I feel it. But I want to find somebody in this strange village of small houses, huge flowers and many suns before I wake up."

Nick was going through the air with difficulty. The air was very dense in spite of its tender transparency. The day was hot. Nick came to one of the houses.

He began to discern the silhouettes of people who were in the yard of the house. The silhouettes had different colors. It looked as if a beautiful rainbow had separated into several colored lines which became the silhouettes of people. People were friendly to each other. He saw that they were having a talk but Nick could not hear the words of the talk. Otherwise, Nick was convinced that he knew the subject of their talk.

"Who is this man?" One colored person asked another. "He is a transparent person without any concrete color."

Nick was very confused because he understood that the words were said about him.

"Am I a transparent man without any colors? It is an interesting dream, but I do not want to be such a man."

Nick's recollections heard those words too. Therefore, they began to play their music in Nick's soul.

"Oh! Please, look at the man!" The silhouettes

cried to each other. "The man is beginning to change. You can see some little colored lights in his transparent figure. How beautiful it is!" They cried again.

From that moment the air of the village allowed Nick to become part of the village. He might go along the streets without difficulty. He was like a little boat which drifted along the street. Nick heard many joyful talks of colored silhouettes. Suddenly he saw the face of his mother that was painted by a beautiful cloud. The big cloud was flying above his head. Usually clouds bring coolness and rain. That cloud was giving the warmth through the face of his mother which was painted on the cloud.

"I forgot many important events of my childhood," Nick thought. "If my soul is so gray and dull, then it is my guilt. I should care about my spiritual world," he decided.

Many little bells rang up in the village when Nick accepted that solution. Every sun above the houses became brighter. The cloud disappeared. But a light rain started though the sky had no clouds. A little later the rain was so fairly general that Nick had not a chance to see the houses or colored silhouettes. Then, the rain stopped. Nick was standing on the big green field of the colored flowers. He was alone.

Nick forgot his dream after he woke up. The next evening he was watching a movie on TV. The usual glass of red wine was set before him on the table.

The song

Tom was going along the street. He was very tired and sad. He could not understand what he should do so that his mood could be improved.

Tom had a look at the big empty sky. The answer did not exist in the sky either. His wonderful woman who was the unique woman for him was lost for him. She had told him that she did not love him anymore. He had not any job. He had no true friends. Tom had not a chance to tell anybody about his mood. It was a gray evening. People were thinking about their own problems. Every person had many problems in life. Often we do not think about other people because our problems are like a spiritual cage for us. We create the cage by ourselves. It is an easy way to see all the problems when they are enclosed in the space of a cage. But it is difficult to leave the cage of our problems once we have entered it. So, Tom was in the transparent cage of his problems. People were going along the street with the burden of their own cages too.

Tom went to the bank of the river. The autumn water of the river was cold. The black color of the water could not bring any consolation for him. The river was thinking about the dirt. A big factory had dumped the dirt in the river several days before. The river was feeling that the fish that were the children of the river were very ill because of that dirt.

"They can die," the river thought. "I will stay alone. Is my life necessary for me if I stay alone? No. The sky loves me. The sky loves to look at me like a mirror. I often feel the reflection of the sky into my water. But

I do not want to be only an empty mirror for the sky. I need my funny children that are the fish."

The river had its own cage of serious problems. The river did not notice Tom's face while he had a look at its water. Therefore, he did not receive the consolation by the beautiful strong river either. The birds were sleeping at that moment. The night came into the city. Black sky, black water of the river and black color of all things that Tom saw around him. He cried. He was so lonely under the high sky in the black night. It was a huge grief of loneliness in a city that was full of so many people. Darkness came into Tom's feelings. The cage and the darkness… He felt that it was too much for him.

The darkness told him, "Please, listen to me. I will calm you down. I know how wonderful the feeling of nothing is. It is the darkness. It is me. I will relieve your pain. I will help you Tom."

Tom was inside the black space of the black words. He had no chance to resist the darkness. Tom went to the river again. He put his hands inside the cold water.

"Probably it would be a wonderful feeling of calmness if my body could be taken by this cold river. I would forget all my problems. I would be free."

The river was sleeping at that time. He entered the cold water. He was ready to become a piece of the water. Tom was sure that it was the unique solution for his problems.

Suddenly he heard a beautiful song. The song flew to him from the opened window of one of the flats in a building. It dissolved the darkness around Tom. It was a very tender song from the days of his childhood. It was the song of his mother. Often she sang this song to him when he was a little boy. He remembered how he was asking his mother to sing this song when he was going to sleep. Tom had wonderful night dreams because of it.

Who told that tenderness is not strong?

Tom returned to the bank of the river. He cried. "My mother died many years ago, but I am sure that my mother is not far from me now. She loves me. I must be strong. I must live because I will stay in dark space forever if

I die now. I cannot meet my mother in that space," Tom thought.

He opened the cage of his problems. He came to light. He was free.

In two years Tom fell in love with a beautiful girl They married. They had two children, a boy and a girl. The daughter was named after his mother.

The old mirror

I would like to be far away from this world. I think I could create another harmonic world that would be a beautiful world for me," the old man thought sadly.

He was sitting in front of a big old mirror. His father had bought that mirror many years ago. The old man recollected his childhood when the trees were like unknown people. They were the piece of the garden where he liked to walk every day. It was a big country of the beautiful aromas, sounds and birds. He liked to be inside that world of the colored tale, which was a reality for him in the days of his childhood. Also the old man recollected that every day was like a little life for him. He did not think about the death or illness. He did not think about bad events. That world opened the doors of gladness and happiness for him. The old man remembered that he was a funny young boy with fair hair. His mother loved to stroke his fair hair. She often told him that his hair was like a tender silk.

The wonderful old mirror has been hung in her room when she was celebrating her birthday. It was a warm sunny day. The old man could recollect every minute of that day. It was a very happy day of his childhood.

He remembered that his father had brought the mirror into the room.

"I wish you, my dear, that you could always see what a beautiful woman you are."

The father told his mother. His mother burst out laughing and kissed him.

The mirror became a favorite thing in the house. It was like another world that was keeping their smiles, hopes and wonderful emotions inside it. The mirror kept their reflections and emotions forever. Now the old man was staring at the mirror.

"Where is the reflection of my beautiful young mother? Where are her gladness and beauty of her eyes? She died many years ago, but I need to find her. Maybe it is madness? Maybe… But the mirror took our reflections. Therefore, it maybe possible to take them back," the old man thought.

"Yesterday I was in a strange dream my mother told me that I could find her in our old mirror. But I can see only myself". The old man cried.

He was very lonely at that moment. It was so hard feeling for him that the old man decided to remove the mirror from the wall where it had hung so many years. He took the mirror in his hands.

Suddenly he felt that a little piece of paper existed behind the mirror. The old man turned the mirror back to front. A little piece of paper was hidden behind the back of the mirror. He unfolded the paper and began to read.

"I love you, my precious son. I love you, my beautiful boy. You are the best boy in the world. If I die, you should remember that I will always love you in any world of unknown space of death."

It was the words by his beautiful mother. The old man might recognize them among thousands of words.

The old man became calm. He hung up the mirror on the wall. From that day he was sure that the world was a wonderful world and his mother was always near him.

A journey

Richard recollected days of his childhood, "I lived with my beautiful young parents in a big house. They loved each other. They loved me. Trees were high. My parents had a beautiful huge garden with flowers. Also I remember a river. It was so wonderful when we had a walk by the river. The high sky was flying above us. And I remember long streets. There were many big houses lining broad streets. It was a special space of gladness, love and happiness for me."

Richard's recollections were a spiritual support to him. His life was not easy. He had many problems. Only his recollections did not betray him. Often Richard recollected a beautiful young girl who liked to wear a bright red dress. She always smiled to him. She was so charming that flowers in her hands had less beauty than the girl.

"Maybe she was born on another planet? She simply forgot to tell me about it. Maybe…" Richard thought. "I must come back in the city of my childhood. I must see the big streets and the beautiful garden of my parents. Maybe I could find the girl too? My parents died many years ago. Probably the house is empty now."

One day Richard took a trip to the town where he lived many years ago.

"It is like I am going inside my recollections. I am sure it will heal me."

Richard left the train. He decided to find the street where his parents' house used to stand a long time before. Richard was in a wonderful mood.

Although he was surprised to see that the streets were very old and very narrow. All the houses, which were standing along the streets, were very small too. They were not very beautiful.

Richard asked a woman who was standing in front of her old house about the house of his parents.

"I will help you," the woman said. "At present time another family lives in this house. I remember the nice funny boy with large gray eyes who lived in this house many years ago. But he lives in another city now. I will never forget him," the woman said sadly.

Richard looked at the woman attentively. Suddenly he realized that she was the girl from the days of his childhood. She was the girl of Richard's dreams.

But the woman was calm and tired. She was not like the girl from his recollections. And she was not born on another planet. The woman was an ordinary woman.

"I can not believe in it. I am sure that it is a mistake." Richard thought.

He was going to the train that was like a friend for him.

The train would help him to leave the town. Richard decided to keep calm during the way. It was important for Richard because he was beginning to realize that he had lost something very important in his life. But he was upset again when he saw a small river with old bridge across the river. He feared he would be mad if he didn't find a way to feel better.

His solution was simple, "It is not the river of my childhood. I will not believe it. It is another river. I will forget this journey. My life is not easy. I will not be able to survive if I lose the world of my recollections. Now I will not go to the house of my parents. Let this house remain a big and beautiful house in my memory. Let the garden remain the huge beautiful garden. I need it. It is my spiritual world which will always be the reality for me by my recollections. Yes, I will forget this journey."

He was going along a small old street. He was so sad that he did not realize that he was going to the house of his parents instead of taking the road to the train. Drops of the rain began to play their tender soft music on the leaves of old trees.

Suddenly Richard heard somebody calling him. He looked at the old house. Richard saw the beautiful huge garden around that house. A man and a woman were standing on the porch of the old house. They were smiling to him and giving a wave.

The day of the meeting

A bouquet of blue flowers in a big transparent vase was set on the porch of an old house. Bright different butterflies were flying in the rooms of the house. The day was created in a space of warmth.

It was a special day. The day of the meeting...

Every person in the city would have a meeting with another person who was for each one the most precious person being but had left this world.

All the people were very calm on that day. They knew that they could go anywhere. They could do any work. The possibility of the meeting did not depend on it. It would happen whatever their life conditions.

Every person had a dream in which a strange house with a blue bouquet standing on the porch and beautiful different butterflies in the rooms were shown to the person.

All the citizens of the city were calm in the morning. Every person thought that the dream was a special. Therefore, they did not tell anybody about that strange dream. They were waiting for the meeting. People in their apartments, people in the streets, people in the shops waited for the meeting with the persons who were so precious for them. They began to worry in the evening because the time for the meeting became too short. The night stood before every door in the city.

"Perhaps it was a joke of my dream," people thought while lying in bed late in the evening of that day.

Night had opened its black eyes and the city's space became a dark quiet space. People slept. They were in their dreams. The spaces of thoughts, hopes and unknown worlds were mixed with the night. And every person came into each one's a unique house of many light rooms where different colored butterflies were flying in. The sun was bright.

It was the day of the meeting which was promised in the previous dream. People did not understand the night message because they were used to thinking in terms of usual events and conditions. The day must be at the time of day. It was difficult to believe that the day could happen at nighttime.

People were going through different rooms. The rooms were full of the deep emotions and wonderful thoughts by people who had left a usual world. It was so strange to move inside the space of emotions and thoughts. Sometimes it was reminding of cold water. Sometimes it was like a fresh wind that kissed the cheek. Sometimes it was like a sad autumn rain. People felt that space although no word was said to them. They understood that they were going to the place of the meeting.

So, they came into the last room. Certainly they came into the last room at a different time. It depended on the number of rooms in the house where every person was. It depended on the time which was needed for different persons for being in the rooms of the houses. The beautiful blue bouquet was in the center of the last room... A ray of the sun was like a tender smile of the precious person who had left a usual world of people.

"Now we are able to stay calm and happy the next days of our life thanks to this day of the meeting," people thought in the morning.

It may seem a strange thing but nobody spoke about the dream. Colorful butterflies were flying from early morning to the late evening during that day. People were smiling to them and were keeping the secret. The space of the city was full of recollections. Yes, it was a day of recollections. It was a day of a sureness for the future meeting.

Contents

The story "The main words" was first published in "The World Healing Book" ISBN: 9789979953111. The 14th Dalai Lama participated in this book. The American poets Lawrence Ferlinghetti and Rita Dove are also participants of the project. The project has brought together more then 150 poets, religious leaders, artists and thinkers from around the world. The simple wish for peace in the heart and in the world.

Lightning Source UK Ltd.
Milton Keynes UK
UKHW020647160822
407375UK00009B/574

9 798210 520630